This story was inspired by Gemma, Antonia Barber's adopted Vietnamese daughter. Gemma lives in the country with her mother, who wrote this story; her older brothers, Jonathan and Nicholas; their dog, Bracken; three cats, Dinah, Sam and Simon; a pond full of goldfish and a big garden where the chickens wander all day long.

For Gina *AB*
For Jeannaret *KL*

Text copyright © 1992 by Antonia Barber.
Illustrations copyright © 1992 by Karin Littlewood.
All rights reserved. Published by Scholastic Inc.,
by arrangement with ABC, All Books for Children,
a division of The All Children's Company Ltd.,
33 Museum Street, London, WC1A 1LD, England.
SCHOLASTIC HARDCOVER is a registered trademark of Scholastic Inc.

Library of Congress Cataloging-in-Publication Data
Barber, Antonia.
Gemma and the baby chick / by Antonia Barber; illustrated by Karin Littlewood.
p. cm.
Summary: Gemma, who collects eggs from the henhouse, discovers a hen
sitting on her eggs and helps save a chick that is slow to hatch.
ISBN 0-590-45479-X
[1. Eggs—Fiction. 2. Chickens—Fiction. 3. Farm life—Fiction.]
I. Littlewood, Karin, ill. II. Title.
PZ7.B2323Ge 1993
[E]—dc20   91-36550
                                                 CIP
                                                 AC

12 11 10 9 8 7 6 5 4 3 2 1   3 4 5 6 7 8/9
Printed in Hong Kong
First Scholastic printing, March 1993

Gemma and the Baby Chick

Written by Antonia Barber · *Illustrated by* Karin Littlewood

SCHOLASTIC INC. · NEW YORK

Gemma came home from school and went to feed the chickens. There were seventeen gray, speckled hens and one fine cock with long tail feathers. All day long they scratched around the farm, eating up the worms and insects.

They were waiting as usual by the barn door,
crowding around as Gemma scattered the
golden grains. She took the egg basket
and went down to the henhouse.

Gemma lifted the lid of the nest-box and found
a hen sitting on the eggs. She tried to slip
her hand under the warm feathers,
but the hen turned her head
sharply and pecked her.

Gemma found her mother in the kitchen, cracking eggs into a blue bowl to make a cake. "There's a hen sitting on the eggs and she pecked me."

"Perhaps she's gone broody. Did it hurt?"

"Not much. What does 'broody' mean?"

"She may be hatching some chicks. I'll come and look." Together they went out into the fine spring day.

The hen in the nest-box was staring straight ahead. She pecked at them crossly and would not move.

Gemma helped her mother fetch the broody coop from the
barn. The broody coop was a tiny henhouse just big enough
for one hen, with a wire netting run fixed to the front. Then
they made a straw nest inside and lined it with soft hay.

"Now we must put the hen and her eggs into the coop. If we don't, she'll steal all the other hens' eggs and she won't be able to keep them all warm."

"Watch," said Gemma's mother. "This is the part she won't like." She pinned down the hen's wings as she lifted her. The hen screeched, and all the other hens took up the cry. "Hen stealers!" they clucked. "Egg robbers!"

The old cock hurried up bravely. But he saw only
the woman who fed him each morning and the girl who
scattered corn in the afternoon. He paused, uncertain.

The hen flapped about, shrieking in the little run.
She did not seem to notice the eggs.

"Leave her," said Gemma's mother. "By the time
our cake is done, she will have settled down."

Gemma's mother was right. When the hot cake
was on the wire rack, Gemma found the broody
hen sitting tight on her precious eggs.

For three long weeks, the hen sat there. Gemma went to see her every day. Even when Gemma stroked her, the hen did not move or peck.

"She seems to be under a magic spell," said Gemma.

"The eggs have cast their spell on her," said her mother.

One day the hen started to make soft calling noises.

Gemma's mother said, "She can hear the chicks. She is telling the slow ones to hurry so that they'll all hatch together."

Gemma's mother took an egg from the nest . . .

. . . and Gemma listened. It was
warm, and a busy chirping came from
inside. Could the chicks hear one another?
Was it like talking in bed after the light was out?

   "What happens if one is late?" she asked. She was
often late herself.

   Her mother smiled. "Wait and see."

The next morning, Gemma got up very early and hurried out. She knew at once that the chicks had hatched. The hen was clucking over a crowd of fluffy balls that ran around her feet. Gemma had expected the chicks to be bright yellow, but these were gray with yellow markings.

It was hard to count the chicks as they scurried about, but Gemma thought there should be more.

In the nest, amid the broken eggshells, she found three eggs. She took one out, but it was cold and silent. Was it empty? Or was there a chick inside that had been too late and was now dying of cold? She gathered up the eggs and ran back to the house. Her mother was writing at the kitchen table.

"The hen hatched seven chicks," said Gemma, "but some of them were late." A small tear trickled down her cheek.

Her mother brushed away the tear. "Let's see what we can do." She filled the blue mixing bowl with warm water. Carefully she put the eggs in, and one by one they floated to the top.

"Watch," said her mother. "This is the magic part."

Slowly the warmth of the water seeped through the cold shells. Then suddenly one of the eggs tipped over onto its side and then back upright.

"Oh!" said Gemma. "It moved by itself!"

The egg rocked from side to side. It made a tiny cheeping sound.

"You saved it just in time," said her mother. "If we keep it warm, it will hatch by morning."

Gemma put an old sweater into the basket and tucked the egg into the soft folds and carried the chirping egg to the warm cabinet by the boiler. When bedtime came, the chick had begun to tap on the inside of the shell. "Go to sleep," said her mother. "I'll wake you when the time comes."

Gemma was dreaming when
she felt her mother shaking her
gently. "Wake up," she said.
"The chick is hatching."

They sat on the landing by
the cabinet and watched the egg.
The chick had begun to crack
the shell from inside. Gemma
thought the egg looked lonely.
She felt that someone should
be loving the chick when it
came out into a strange
world. "Can I hold it?"
she whispered.

Her mother put the egg into her hands and they sat in silence, watching while the rest of the house slept. It seemed to Gemma that they shared the greatest secret in the world. Then the lining split and out came a big yellow claw. It was so unexpected and the egg looked so funny with just one leg sticking out, that they both began to laugh.

The chick gave a loud chirp and stretched itself suddenly. The egg fell apart and out came not a pretty round ball of fluff, but a wet, gawky little chick, all beak and claws.

Gemma stared in wonder at the odd little creature that sat in the palm of her hand. And then she smiled. "That," she told her mother, "is the cutest, funniest little chick I have ever seen." Her mother kissed her. She put the chick back into the sweater. "It needs to be warm while it's drying. Then we must give it back to the hen." "Couldn't I keep it for my very own?"

But Gemma's mother told her that the hen would care for her chicks every moment. "You will be at school; think how lonely your chick would be without brothers or sisters or a mother to look after it."

"Can I keep it for a day or two?"

"The hen can tell by the smell of them which are her own chicks. She will chase any other chicks away. I must slip this chick underneath her feathers now, while she's sleeping. Then, by morning, it will smell like all the others, and she will look after it."

"Can I come with you?"

Her mother hugged her. "Of course."

The dry chick was fluffy and pretty.
Gemma carried it in the basket. It was
an adventure to be creeping down to
the henhouse in her nightgown in the
moonlit darkness.

"Do you want to put the chick under
the hen," asked her mother, "or will you
hold the flashlight for me?"

"I'll do it." She wanted to make the
gift herself.

Gemma took the chick from the basket,
kissed it lightly, then tucked it into the nest of
soft hay. For a moment it was caught in the bright
light. Then it burrowed through the hen's feathers and
was gone, seeking the warm and comfortable darkness.

Gemma and her mother walked back through the warm darkness. Each was busy with her own thoughts. All the trees seemed full of sleeping birds. Only one bird was still awake, and they paused for a moment before they went in to listen to the nightingale singing in the birch trees on the far side of the pond.